Sparkling Steps

Biba—our chatty tortie-tabby girl.

GROSSET & DUNLAP
Published by the Penguin Group
Penguin Group (USA) Inc., 375 Hudson Street,
New York, New York 10014, USA
Penguin Group (Canada), 90 Eglinton Avenue East, Suite 700,
Toronto, Ontario M4P 2Y3, Canada
(a division of Pearson Penguin Canada Inc.)
Penguin Books Ltd., 80 Strand, London WC2R 0RL, England
Penguin Group Ireland, 25 St. Stephen's Green, Dublin 2, Ireland
(a division of Penguin Books Ltd.)
Penguin Group (Australia), 250 Camberwell Road, Camberwell, Victoria 3124,
Australia (a division of Pearson Australia Group Pty. Ltd.)
Penguin Books India Pvt. Ltd., 11 Community Centre, Panchsheel Park,
New Delhi—110 017, India
Penguin Group (NZ), 67 Apollo Drive, Rosedale, North Shore 0632,
New Zealand (a division of Pearson New Zealand Ltd.)
Penguin Books (South Africa) (Pty.) Ltd., 24 Sturdee Avenue,
Rosebank, Johannesburg 2196, South Africa

Penguin Books Ltd., Registered Offices:
80 Strand, London WC2R 0RL, England

Library of Congress Control Number: 2009017631

ISBN 978-0-448-45063-6 10 9 8 7 6 5 4 3 2

Sparkling Steps

SUE BENTLEY

Illustrated by Angela Swan

Grosset & Dunlap

★ Prologue ★

A terrifying growl sounded close by and Flame, the young, white lion, froze. He had hoped it was safe to return this time. But he was wrong. He knew he needed to act quickly.

Sparks ignited in Flame's fur and there was a flash of bright white light. Where he had stood now crouched a tiny kitten with a round face and velvety, blue-gray fur.

An old, gray lion limped forward from the shadows at the back of the cave. "Prince Flame! You shouldn't be here. You must hide!"

"There is no time, Cirrus. Uncle Ebony is coming!" the little kitten meowed, trembling.

Cirrus reached out a large paw and gently drew the kitten behind a pile of rocks to hide.

A loud scraping sound pierced the cave. Flame's heart beat fast in his little chest as he listened to Ebony sharpening his claws on a rock. A flash of anger glittered in the tiny kitten's emerald eyes. "One day I will take back the throne my uncle stole from me!" he meowed bravely.

"And I do not doubt that you will be a wise ruler, my prince," Cirrus said, a smile creasing his wrinkled muzzle. He gave Flame's tiny head an affectionate lick.

A menacing shape almost filled the cave's entrance. Raising its powerful head, the enormous, black lion shook its mane. Ebony growled again. Peering into the cave, he sniffed the air. "Who's there? Show yourselves!" he roared.

"Go, Flame!" Cirrus urged through worn teeth. "Go quickly! Use your kitten disguise and hide in the other world. Return again when you have grown strong and powerful!"

Silver sparks glittered in Flame's blue-gray fur. The tiny kitten meowed as he felt the power building inside him. He felt himself falling. Falling . . .

Chapter ★ONE★

"I'm here! I'm actually at Yew Lodge!" Olivia Goddard whispered excitedly to herself, as she entered the changing rooms.

Everywhere she looked, there were unfamiliar girls in gray skirts, white blouses, and blue cardigans. Olivia found a space and started taking her things out of her bag. She had just changed into her new, pink leotard when a group of girls walked in, giggling and whispering to each other. They looked about ten years old, the same as Olivia.

A small girl with silver-blond hair and blue eyes stood nearest to Olivia.

Olivia smiled. "Hi, I'm new here. I think I'm in your class," she said.

"So what?" the blond girl said rudely. She looked up at Olivia and smirked. "What's the weather like up there?"

There were more muffled giggles and whispers from the other girls.

Olivia was used to being teased about her height. "I don't know. My head's in the clouds," she joked. "What's it like down there?"

"She told you, Lucy!" one of the other girls said with a chuckle as Lucy scowled and turned away.

The door banged as a girl with a

mop of bright red hair came running into the changing room. She dumped her bag on the bench next to Olivia. "Phew! Just made it. The bus was late," she puffed. She gave Olivia a big grin. "Serves me right, for not living here like everyone else, I guess! Hi, I'm Tamsin!"

"Hi, I'm Olivia," Olivia said, smiling.

Tamsin was thin with pale skin and

freckles. She smelled of fresh air and spearmint chewing gum.

"Welcome to Yew Lodge!" Tamsin dragged a creased leotard and a pair of wrinkled, white ankle socks out of her bag. "Are you a day girl, like me?"

"No, I'm boarding," Olivia replied. "My mom's just dropped me off. I haven't even had time to unpack properly, but I didn't want to miss my first class. It feels a little weird to be starting midterm."

"I bet it does," Tamsin agreed. "Have you met any of the others yet?"

"Only Lucy, but she wasn't exactly friendly," Olivia said quietly.

Tamsin rolled her eyes. "What a surprise. Not!" she whispered back.

"Lucy Castor thinks she's Miss Perfect. Don't pay any attention to her."

Olivia laughed, happy to see that not everyone was so unfriendly.

Unfortunately, Lucy chose that moment to walk by on her way to the studio.

"Ooh, look, Mariko!" she said to the pretty girl with high cheekbones and almond eyes by her side. "Beanpole and Frizz are friends."

Olivia's heart sank as she noticed Tamsin's face flush before she twisted her mass of curly, red hair into a bun.

"I think you've got amazing hair," Olivia said, hoping that Lucy's mean comment hadn't scared off the only girl to be friendly to her so far.

"Thanks, Olivia," Tamsin said with a wry chuckle. "I guess it is a bit of a frizz—I have to use tons of this gel stuff to stop bits of it from popping out and hanging in my eyes."

Olivia, relieved to see that Tamsin hadn't been too bothered by Lucy, groaned in sympathy. "My hair does that, too."

Tamsin held out the tube of hair gel. "Try some of this."

"Thanks." Olivia squeezed some out and smoothed it on to her thick brown hair. In no time at all, she had coiled it around and pinned it into a neat bun. She sat down to tie her shoelaces.

Tamsin was tying hers, too. "Don't forget to tuck in the ends. Miss Frances hates flapping laces. She calls them pig's ears!" she said. A few minutes later, she jumped up. "I'm done. Ready?"

Olivia nodded.

As she followed Tamsin into the large, light studio with its shiny, wooden floor, Olivia felt her stomach clench with nerves. Three entire walls were mirrored and a double barre ran around them. In one corner, a woman was seated at a piano.

"Here's Miss Frances," Tamsin whispered as the teacher came in.

Olivia stared at the tiny, straight-backed woman. Frances Edwards had been a principal dancer with a famous ballet company. There was a photo of her dancing in *Giselle* in Olivia's ballet book, which had been a present for her tenth birthday.

"Good morning, class. Let's begin," said Miss Frances, giving a signal to the pianist. Olivia and Tamsin faced the barre and, along with everyone else, began doing pliés in time to the music.

Olivia felt herself relaxing as she concentrated on the familiar exercises. She had been doing these movements since she was four years old. She knew that even the greatest dancers did them, too, every single day.

Miss Frances walked around, adjusting the placement of a dancer's arm or leg. When she reached Olivia, she frowned. She made a chopping motion in the air and the piano stopped abruptly. "You!

Come out here," she said sharply.

Olivia swallowed as she walked into the center of the studio.

"You're new, right? What's your name?" Miss Frances asked.

"Olivia Goddard," Olivia answered. "It . . . it's my first day."

"Then why didn't you come and introduce yourself?" The teacher's stern eyes raked Olivia's face. "It's very bad manners to just slip into my class without a word."

"Slip into class? Gallop like a giraffe is more like it!" Lucy Castor snickered from where she was standing.

Olivia tried to pretend she hadn't heard. "I'm sorry, Miss Frances. I . . . I just didn't think," she stammered, her face scarlet.

"Okay. Let's forget about it. Where did you take ballet lessons?" asked Miss Frances more gently.

Olivia told her and explained that she had been taking ballet lessons twice a week.

Miss Frances nodded slowly. "Well, you're going to have two classes a day now. So be prepared to work hard. You'll find ballet school to be very challenging."

"I hope so, Miss Frances. That's why I came here," Olivia said spiritedly.

Miss Frances's sharp eyes flashed with approval. "Okay. Go back to the barre. I want to see you dance."

Olivia went to the barre and took up a basic position. It felt like everybody was watching her, especially Lucy and Mariko. Tamsin caught her eye and gave her a thumbs-up sign.

As Miss Frances gave her instructions, Olivia took a deep breath and began. After a few minutes, she felt the love of dancing sweep through her and she forgot to be self-conscious. By the time Miss Frances told her to stop, she was hot and sweaty and her muscles were tingling.

"You have style, but your technique could be improved," Miss Frances said seriously. "Take a rest now. Get a towel to wipe your face."

"Yes, Miss Frances," Olivia said numbly, as she went back into the changing room. She had tried her best, but it seemed she had a long way to go before she impressed Miss Frances.

Olivia went to the sinks and splashed her face with cold water as she thought about what a difficult morning it had been all around. Yew Lodge seemed really different from the exciting place she had always dreamed about.

Olivia sighed, drying her face on a towel. Suddenly a bright silver flash from

out of the corner of her eye stopped her in her tracks.

Olivia whirled around. "Oh," she gasped, blinking hard.

At the far end of the room crouched a tiny, fluffy, blue-gray kitten with a round face and the most enormous emerald green eyes Olivia had ever seen. Its fur and whiskers seemed to glitter with thousands of tiny stars.

Olivia rubbed her face with the towel again—she'd obviously danced too hard and was seeing things now! She looked up from the towel. The sparkles had disappeared, but the kitten was still there. Perhaps it belonged to the lodge.

She bent down. "Hello, aren't you gorgeous? Don't be scared. I won't hurt you," she crooned gently, reaching out her hand. "What's your name, then?"

"My name is Prince Flame," the kitten meowed. "Can you help me, please?"

Chapter *TWO*

Olivia almost toppled over. She jerked her hand back and stared at the kitten in complete shock.

"Did . . . did you really just speak?" she gasped, looking around wildly to see if anyone was hiding nearby. She wouldn't put it past Lucy to play a trick on her.

The fluffy kitten was trembling all over, but it sat up straight and pricked up its ears. Despite its tiny size it didn't seem to be afraid of her. "Yes, I did. I am Flame, heir to the Lion Throne. Who are you?"

"I'm . . . um, Olivia Goddard," Olivia stammered, her curiosity beginning to get the better of her shock. "Where did you come from?"

"I am in disguise," Flame meowed softly. "I come from another world, far from here."

"What? Like from outer space? But if . . . if you're disguised as a kitten, what are you re—" Olivia began and then stopped as a scary thought occurred to her. Maybe Flame was really an alien, with warty skin and millions of octopus arms! "Wait! Maybe I don't want to know . . . !" she gabbled.

But it was too late. There was another flash, so bright this time that for a moment Olivia couldn't see a thing. She rubbed her eyes. When she looked again, she saw that where the tiny kitten had crouched now stood a regal, young lion with glittering white fur.

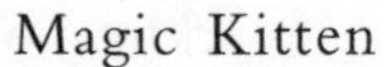

Olivia backed away in amazement. "Flame?"

The lion looked at Olivia with its emerald eyes and nodded slowly. But before she could say anything else, he vanished in a shower of sparkles and appeared once more as a tiny, fluffy, blue-gray kitten.

"Wow! You really are a lion prince!" Olivia gasped, relieved and impressed at the same time. "But why would you need my help?"

Flame gave a small, shaky meow. "My uncle Ebony. He is very powerful and has stolen my throne. He rules in my place and sends his spies to search for me and kill me."

"Kill you?" Olivia asked, horrified.

"Yes. I must hide. Will you help me, Olivia?"

Olivia's heart went out to the tiny kitten—she knew exactly what it was like to feel all alone. "I'd love to help you, Flame, but pets aren't allowed in ballet school," she said, biting her lip. "I don't even have my own room. There're eight of us in the dormitory. It would be impossible to hide you."

Flame tilted his little, round head. "Not if I made myself invisible. Then no one will see me, except you."

"Really? Well—if you can do that . . ." Olivia came to a decision. She picked Flame up gently and stroked his silky ears. "Okay. You're living with me. I won't let anybody hurt you! The only thing is, I have to go back out soon. My teacher will be wondering where I am, so you'll have to become invisible right away. Is that okay?"

Flame didn't reply, but his whiskers crackled with electricity and his fluffy

blue-gray fur glittered all over with silver sparkles that fizzed against Olivia's hands. She felt a warm tingling sensation down her back. It felt very strange, but not unpleasant.

"It is done. Only you can see me now," Flame purred happily, as the sparks slowly faded away. "Thank you, Olivia."

"You're welcome." Olivia smiled. "I wonder what Tamsin will say when I tell her about you."

Flame stiffened. He stretched up one tiny, blue-gray paw and touched her face.

"No! You must not tell anyone about me."

"Really? I'm sure Tamsin's not like the other girls I've met here. She seems really nice."

"I am sorry." Flame looked up at her, his big, green eyes serious. "You cannot tell anyone about me. Promise, Olivia."

Olivia thought about it. She felt a bit bad for keeping something so amazing from the friendly girl she had met that morning. But if it was the only way that

Flame could stay with her, she knew what she must do.

"All right. I promise," Olivia said. "You'll be my secret. My secret magic kitten!"

Chapter *THREE*

As Olivia went back to the studio, Flame padded along beside her. He spotted the piano and scampered straight over and curled up beneath it. Although Flame was invisible, Olivia couldn't help thinking that someone would notice the tiny, blue-gray kitten. But, after a while, when no one did, she gradually relaxed.

Olivia saw that Miss Frances was coaching Tamsin. "Concentrate! Keep your legs tight and don't sway backward, Tamsin. Think of an imaginary line from the top of your head down to your toe."

Olivia stood and watched as Tamsin lifted one arm and leg in the melting, flowing movements of *battement fondu*. She was impressed. Tamsin was poised and elegant and could lift her pointed toe above the second barre.

"What are you staring at? Didn't they do real dancing where you come from, Beanpole?" Lucy hissed in Olivia's ear.

Mariko snickered. "They probably still wear clogs!"

Feeling much braver, now that she had Flame for a friend, Olivia gave the mean girls a fierce look. "I've never worn clogs. But I wish I was wearing them right now!"

Mariko and Lucy moved away warily.

Miss Frances finished coaching Tamsin. "Everyone choose partners," she said. "You'll work together for the rest of the class. Olivia, you will work with Tamsin."

Olivia glanced over at Flame. He was watching her every move with alert, green eyes. She couldn't help wondering what

Miss Frances would say if she knew that there was a magic kitten in her class!

At eleven AM, when class was over, all the girls faced Miss Frances and bowed in a graceful *révérence.*

There was a buzz of noise as everyone filed out. "Are you coming?" Tamsin called to Olivia.

"In a minute," Olivia said, pretending to fiddle with her shoelace. When everyone had left, she went and picked Flame up. "Did you enjoy watching your first ballet class?" she asked him.

His forehead wrinkled in a puzzled frown. "It was interesting, but I found those movements very strange. Are you training to be a warrior, Olivia?" he purred.

Olivia laughed. "No! I want to be a ballerina."

Flame blinked. "What is a *ball-er-ina*?"

"A very special kind of dancer. You get to wear amazing costumes and dance on stage in front of lots of people," Olivia explained simply. "I've got an amazing book with tons of photos of dancers. I'll show you sometime."

"I would like that," Flame meowed.

In the changing room, Flame sat licking his paws under the bench, invisible to all the other girls in Olivia's class.

"We have normal lessons now, until the afternoon dance class," Tamsin told Olivia, zipping up her gray skirt. "I'll see you in the classroom? I just have to go to the bathroom."

"Okay," Olivia called after her. She crouched down to the bench and lowered her voice to a whisper. "It might be better if you get into my school bag, Flame. It could look weird if I look like I'm carrying something that no one can see!"

"That is a good idea." Flame jumped into the open bag.

"I guess you're feeling pretty happy

with yourself?" a familiar voice behind her said.

Olivia didn't bother to look up. She carried on making Flame comfortable among the books and ballet kit. "What are you talking about, Lucy?"

"Don't act dumb! I saw you hanging around in the studio, so you could suck up to Miss Frances!" Lucy cried.

"That's not true! I was waiting for . . . for . . ." Olivia tailed off, realizing that she had been about to mention Flame.

Lucy's eyes flashed with temper. "See! You can't deny it! You're just trying to be a teacher's pet!" Her arm shot out and she grabbed Olivia's school bag.

"Hey! Give that back!" Olivia shouted.

But Lucy had already run away. She

drew back her arm and hurled the bag across the changing room.

"No!" Olivia gave a horrified gasp as her bag, with Flame inside, flew high into the air.

She ran forward in a desperate attempt to catch the soaring bag, but then stopped suddenly as a familiar, warm tingling sensation ran up her spine.

Something strange was about to happen—and Flame was definitely involved!

Olivia watched in amazement as the school bag seemed to slow down. It came to a dead halt, floating in midair for a heartbeat, before whizzing back toward Lucy. Smack! It hit her in the chest.

"Oof!" Lucy lost her balance and sat

down hard on a bench. The girls' coats fell off their pegs and all landed on Lucy in a big messy pile.

"Aargh! Someone get them off me!" Lucy called, kicking her feet from underneath them.

Olivia quickly grabbed her bag before Lucy could get free, and hurried into the hallway. "Flame! Are you all right?" she said, opening the zip wide.

Flame's bright green eyes gleamed at her from the depths of the bag. "I am fine," he purred.

"Thank goodness!" Olivia breathed. She chuckled to herself as she headed for the classroom. "That was amazing, Flame! You should have seen Lucy's face when my bag hit her!"

A howl of rage rang out as Lucy and Mariko burst into the hallway behind Olivia and Flame. "I don't know what just happened. But I'm going to get that teacher's pet. Just you wait!" Lucy stormed.

Chapter *FOUR*

Over the next week or so, Olivia gradually settled into the school's routine. At first, she found two dance classes a day a real challenge. But the exercises designed to strengthen her feet and ankles, which Miss Frances gave her, helped a lot.

Olivia sat near Tamsin during normal school classes and at lunchtimes. Miss Frances often chose them to partner each other. As the tallest girls in the class, they danced together well. Olivia was starting to enjoy herself much more now that she and Tamsin were becoming good friends.

But as Tamsin wasn't living at Yew Lodge, she went home before dinner every night. Olivia would have missed her a lot more if she hadn't had Flame. She wished like crazy that she could tell Tamsin about the magic kitten, but a promise was a promise.

A week of wet weather kept Olivia and Flame indoors in the evenings. As she didn't like watching TV or playing computer games, Olivia began going to the studio for another practice session. With Flame beside her, she worked harder at her dancing than she had ever done before.

"I will help you, Olivia," Flame said one evening, raising a tiny paw.

A cloud of sparks shot towards Olivia, who was working on her leg extensions.

Suddenly her outstretched leg shot straight up in front of her and almost banged into her nose.

"Flame!" she said reprovingly, trying not to giggle. "Stop that! I have to do this by myself!"

"I am sorry," Flame purred, looking crestfallen. "I did not mean to interfere."

"That's okay. I know you meant well," she said, picking him up and giving him a cuddle. "Come on. I'm finished for tonight, anyway."

On her way up to the dorm, she passed Lucy and Mariko who ignored her as they usually did now—which was fine with Olivia.

"I think you really taught Lucy a lesson," she said to Flame later, as he

curled up beside her on the duvet.

Flame blinked at her. "Maybe, but I would not be too sure of that," he purred sleepily.

*

At the end of class the following day, Tamsin joined Olivia as they filed out of the studio. "Miss Frances is really happy with you," she told her.

Olivia blinked at her. "How can you tell? She hardly says anything to me."

Tamsin grinned. "I know the signs," she said. "She watches you when you're not looking and I even caught her smiling once!"

"Really?" Olivia felt a glow of pride. Maybe all her extra hard work was starting to pay off. She looked down at her feet

where Flame was padding alongside her, invisible to everyone else, and smiled as she thought about how much fun she was having at ballet school now.

Miss Frances raised her voice. "Olivia! After you get changed, I want you to come to the shoe department with me."

Olivia's heart beat fast. This could only mean one thing. She was going to get her very first pair of pointe shoes!

"I knew it! Congratulations!" Tamsin said, giving her a hug back in the changing rooms. "I got my pointe shoes last year. I remember feeling like a real dancer for the first time!"

Olivia waited until everyone had left and then lifted Flame into her school bag. "Let's go and find Miss Frances. This is

so exciting!" she whispered to him.

Flame was fascinated by the shoe department. He jumped up on to the counters and sniffed at the rows of shoes, which were being dyed to match some brightly colored costumes.

Miss Frances supervised while Olivia's feet were measured. Then came the wonderful moment when a cardboard shoebox was lifted down from a shelf. Olivia's heart beat fast as she held the box in her hand. She opened it slowly and took out the beautiful, pale peach, satin shoes, with their printed gold labels and blunt tips.

"You have done very well. It's a special time for a young dancer when she gets her first pair of pointe shoes. Enjoy

this moment, Olivia," Miss Frances said, smiling.

"Thank you. I will," Olivia said, her eyes pricking with tears of pride and happiness.

After checking them for the correct

fit, Olivia was allowed to take her new shoes away. She sat on her bed in the dorm to sew ribbons into them. Flame sat nearby on the window sill, watching her with pricked ears.

Olivia finished sewing and held up a shoe. "Isn't it the most gorgeous thing you've ever seen?" she said admiringly.

Flame leaped on to the bed. He tapped the hard, satin-covered tips with a tiny paw, his bright emerald eyes looking puzzled. "Why do they make you strap these on to your feet? Is it a punishment?"

Olivia laughed and lifted him into her lap. "No! They let us dance on the very tips of our toes, *en pointe*, and make us look light and delicate."

"Humans do some very odd things!" Flame lifted a blue-gray paw and flexed his sharp, little claws. "I would never cover my paws!"

"I think that's very sensible!" Olivia said, grinning to herself as a cute picture of Flame wearing tiny ballet shoes filled her head!

The following day, when she wore

her new shoes in class and began simple exercises at the barre, Olivia felt very grown-up. It would be a long time before she could dance *en pointe* for any length of time, but this was definitely a major step toward her dream of becoming a ballerina!

Chapter *FIVE*

"See you tomorrow, Tamsin!" Olivia waved good-bye to her friend at the school gate and then turned back into the school grounds.

Olivia had brought her ballet book outside with her. It was a gorgeous, warm evening, and she planned to find a quiet place to sit and read it with Flame. She wandered down a flower-bordered path, with him scampering along, whiskers twitching as he sniffed the interesting scents. Every now and then, he pounced on a twig or chased a feather. Suddenly, he gave an eager meow and leaped into the air to chase a bumblebee.

"Make sure it doesn't sting you!" Olivia warned as Flame dived head first into the middle of a patch of yellow pansies, leaving only his fluffy, little back legs and short tail in view. A moment later, he reappeared, his nose dusted with sticky, yellow pollen. "What *do* you look like?" she said, chuckling.

The sunset cast a soft glow onto a long, sloping lawn, with an old stone well in the center. After the recent rain, water had gathered in muddy puddles at the bottom of the slope.

"Perfect!" Olivia sighed happily, as she

settled beside a flower bed on the dry grass at the top.

Flame jumped into her lap and curled up, purring contentedly.

Olivia opened her book and began turning the thick, glossy pages. She knew all the photos by heart, but it was fun showing them to Flame. "This is Darcey Bussell, one of my favorite ballerinas. She's tall, like me," she told him. "Here she is as Princess Aurora in *The Sleeping Beauty*. And this is Sylvie Guillem; she's amazing . . ."

Olivia was so engrossed in her book that she didn't notice Lucy and Mariko coming along the path toward her.

"All by yourself, now that Tamsin's gone home?" Lucy called.

"She doesn't have any friends," said Mariko.

Olivia looked up. "If it's a choice of having no friends or having you two, it's no contest!" she murmured.

Lucy came over and stood, looking down at her. "You think you're so smart, don't you?"

Olivia raised an eyebrow. "Do I get a prize if I get the answer right?"

Lucy's blue eyes narrowed with anger. She leaned down and grabbed the ballet book.

Flame was flicked sideways. He leaped into the air and landed in the middle of a nearby flower bed on all fours. Olivia glanced at Flame to check that he was all right before springing to her feet and facing Lucy.

"Give me my book back, or else!" she demanded.

"Why don't you try and make me?" Lucy taunted, skipping backward. She pretended to drop the book and then caught it by one cover, so that the pages flapped.

"Don't you dare tear it!" Olivia warned. "That book was a present and it cost a lot of money!"

Mariko glanced uncertainly at Lucy. "It does look really expensive. Maybe you should give it back."

"Don't be silly!" Lucy's face lit up with an idea. "Come on!" she called to Mariko, already running down the slope.

The puddles! Olivia groaned, knowing what was coming.

Lucy raised the book high above her head.

Olivia felt a warm tingling down her spine once again. Time seemed to stand still. From where Flame was hidden in the flower bed, she saw a glowing, sparkly cloud rise. A tiny paw appeared and a shimmering blue lightning bolt streaked through the air.

The tiny, blue bolt struck the book, just as Lucy went to zing it into the puddle. The book didn't move. It stuck firmly to Lucy's hand.

"Ooh!" Lucy gasped, almost tottering forward off balance. She shook her hand, trying desperately to let go of it.

"Mariko, help! I can't let go of it!" she gasped.

Mariko reached out and grabbed the other end. She tugged and pulled, but couldn't get it out of Lucy's grip.

Shaking her head, she stepped backward and dragged Lucy and the book with her.

"Hey! Stop pulling me around!" complained Lucy.

"I can't help it! Now I can't let go of it either!" Mariko wailed.

The two of them lumbered around crablike, pushing and pulling as they tried to get their hands unstuck.

Olivia bit back a grin as she sidled over to the flower bed. "How long will they be stuck like that?" she whispered to Flame.

His whiskery, little face peered out at her. "Only until you touch the book."

Tempting as it was to leave them there, Olivia strolled over to Lucy and Mariko and reached for her book. "I think that's mine!"

First Mariko, and then Lucy, pinged backward, just as if they'd bounced off a trampoline. There were two enormous splashes as they both landed flat on their faces in the puddle.

Lucy sat up covered in mud, her silver blond hair drooping like a big cowpat over one eye. "What . . . what just happened?" she babbled.

Mariko staggered out of the puddle, dripping mud. "Just look at me! If you hadn't grabbed that book, this wouldn't have happened!" she grumbled.

"Oh, stop whining and help me up!" Lucy shouted.

"Get up by yourself!" Mariko shouted back.

Olivia left them arguing with each

other. As she walked back up the lawn, chuckling to herself, Flame jumped out of the flower bed and trotted after her, leaving a few telltale blue sparkles crackling behind him.

Chapter *SIX*

"I have good news, everyone," Miss Frances announced in class a few days later. "You're going to be doing the Garland Dance from Act 1 of *The Sleeping Beauty* for the school performance at the end of semester."

Olivia and Tamsin exchanged excited looks.

"*The Sleeping Beauty*'s one of my favorite ballets," Olivia said dreamily.

"Mine, too," Tamsin agreed excitedly. "I wonder what our costumes will be like."

No one could talk about anything else. The excited buzz of conversation became even louder when Miss Frances showed the girls some samples of pastel colored fabric and delicate flower trims.

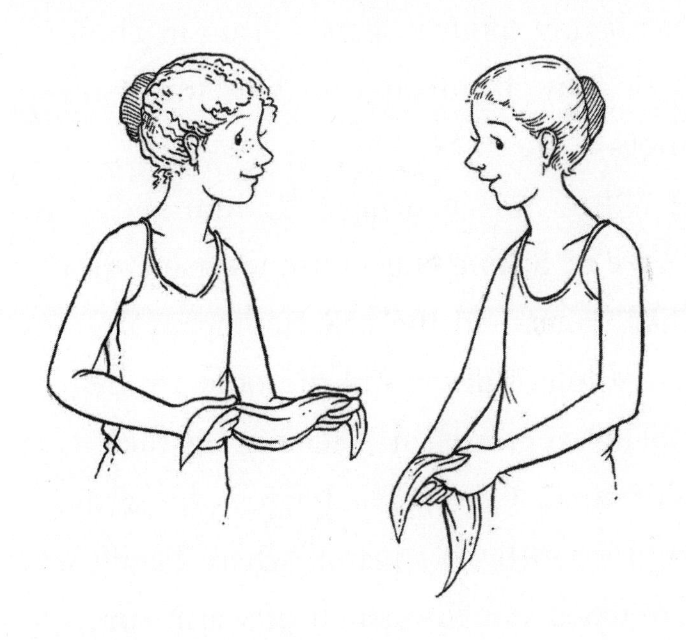

"You may choose the color of your costumes. You'll be wearing classic tutus and matching headdresses made by the wardrobe department," she said with a rare smile.

Everyone gathered around eagerly. Olivia chose a pale oyster silk, trimmed with tiny, pink rosebuds. Tamsin chose pale gray, trimmed with blue forget-me-nots.

"Isn't this amazing?" Tamsin said. "We're having our costumes made, just like dancers in the ballet company!"

While Tamsin and the others were totally engrossed in deciding on their costumes, Olivia sidled across the studio and stood by the piano, where Flame was stretched out in a patch of warm sun.

"Mom and Dad are going to be so proud when they see me in my first ballet school production! I can't wait to call them tonight and tell them all about it!" she whispered to him. "Are you looking forward to it, too?"

Flame had been dozing. He lifted his little head and nodded sleepily. "I hope very much that I will be here to see you dance."

"Be here? Of course you will. Where else would you be?" Olivia asked, confused.

"If my enemies—" Flame began.

"Girls! Get into position to learn the first steps, please." Olivia missed the rest of Flame's reply as Miss Frances's voice carried across the studio.

"I'd better go, Flame. I'll come and get you after class." Olivia bit her lip worriedly as she got into position next to Tamsin. She knew in her heart of hearts that Flame would have to leave one day, but she couldn't bear to even think about it just yet!

Her worries faded gradually as she worked hard to learn the complicated steps for the Garland Dance. Tamsin seemed to get the hang of them quite quickly, but it took Olivia many tries before she got them right.

"Again!" Miss Frances ordered. "The arms are held like this!" She made the students dance the sequence over and over again.

Every movement had to be perfect, the head held just so, the toe pointed at the right angle. Miss Frances was very difficult to please. Usually Olivia loved every second of dance class, but today she was really happy to have normal school classes.

As Olivia bent down at the end of class to let Flame jump into her school bag, she winced a bit.

Flame immediately pricked up his ears. "Is something wrong?" he purred softly.

"It's just my feet. They're a little sore," Olivia said.

Flame meowed with concern. "Should I make the hurt go away?"

Olivia smiled. She had decided not to ask Flame again about when he might leave—he seemed happy to be here with her. "Thanks, Flame," she whispered. "But it's just my body getting used to hard work. As I get stronger it won't hurt as much. It's just part of being a dancer. Don't worry about me. I love it here. I feel like the luckiest girl in the world and I wouldn't change a single thing. And that includes having you here!"

★

After another week of rehearsing to the piano, Miss Frances put on a CD of the beautiful music for the Garland

Dance. Olivia was surprised how different it felt to dance to an orchestra. Now the work of getting the dance perfect started all over again.

The girls had begun to come to class wearing practice tutus, to get used to dancing in costume. One morning, at the end of the class, Olivia was slipping hers off, when Miss Frances called everyone together.

"We shall perform the dance in two rows," Miss Frances told everyone. "In the back row will be . . ." She called out a number of names, including Lucy and Mariko. "And in the front row will be Olivia, Tamsin . . ."

Olivia hardly heard the rest of the names. She couldn't believe it. She was going to dance in the front row!

"Did you hear that, Tamsin? Isn't it amazing?" she said to her friend, as she placed the practice tutu upside down on the special stand in the corner.

Tamsin was drinking from a bottle of water. She wiped her mouth and grinned. "You've worked really hard. You deserve it," she said generously.

"No one's going to be able to see me in the back row, with Beanpole clumping around in front of us!" Lucy complained loudly.

Miss Frances frowned as she turned to Lucy. "The dancers with the best technique will be in the front row. If you want to join them, my advice is to work a lot harder!" she snapped. "Olivia has put in hours of extra practice. Perhaps you should, too."

Lucy's pretty face turned bright red. She walked over to stand beside Mariko.

"I can't stand that teacher's pet. I hope she gets double chickenpox and then I can have her place," she muttered.

Olivia was hurt but she pretended not to hear. No matter what she did or didn't do, Lucy and Mariko were never going to like her. *It's just a fact of life*, she thought, *like having blisters and sore feet, and I just have to get used to it.*

Chapter *SEVEN*

"Only a few days now until the end of the semester. I can't believe how quickly the time's gone. I'm looking forward to seeing you both. Bye, Mom. Give my love to Dad." Olivia hung up the phone after speaking to her parents on Sunday afternoon.

She turned to smile at Flame. "Mom and Dad love to hear all the news. I told them that we've started rehearsing onstage and everything. They're really excited about coming to the school production. I just hope I don't mess up!"

"You will be fine. You are working so hard to be a good dancer," Flame purred.

"Thanks, Flame!" Olivia said, stroking his soft, little ears.

A group of girls from her class walked past. "Hi, Olivia," one of them called. "We're going to watch a video of *The Nutcracker* in the common room. Do you want to come?"

Olivia loved the *Nutcracker* ballet, but she knew she really ought to take Flame outside. He'd spent a lot of time indoors while she had been doing extra practices in the studio. "Thanks, but I think I'll catch up with you later, if that's okay. I'm going outside to get some fresh air," she said to the girls.

"Okay. See you later," they called as they walked off.

"Come on, Flame. I bet you'd love to run around outside."

Flame nodded eagerly as he followed

her out into the school grounds. Olivia strolled past the tennis courts. There was no one playing tennis today. Most students had gone home for the weekend to visit their parents, leaving only the boarders.

It was very quiet on the grounds. Olivia spotted some pink roses in the bed with the yellow pansies. As she stopped to smell one of them, Flame darted past in pursuit of a huge, wood pigeon.

"You've got no chance of catching that," she said, chuckling to herself as he scrambled under a bush after it. The pigeon was as big as he was!

Olivia wandered down the winding path to the sloping lawn with the old well in the center. She sat and watched a squirrel loping across the grass, while she waited for Flame to come and find her.

After five minutes or so, when he hadn't appeared, she went to look for him. "Flame?" she called softly, retracing her steps along the path, peering into flower beds and parting the bushes. "Flame? Where are you?"

There was no answering meow.

Olivia started to feel worried. Where could he be? What if Flame's enemies had found him already? They might have hurt him or worse!

Suddenly she heard a little wail of distress. It was coming from the direction of the lawn, behind her. With her heart racing, Olivia whipped around and dashed back there.

"Oh!" she gasped.

Lucy and Mariko stood in the center of the lawn. Lucy had both hands tightly wrapped around Flame's middle. His bottom half was dangling in midair.

Flame must have been so engrossed in

playing with the wood pigeon that he had forgotten to stay invisible! Now he couldn't do any magic without giving himself away.

"Stop wriggling!" Lucy said crossly, squeezing harder, as Flame gave another howl and lashed his tiny tail.

Olivia had had just about enough of Lucy and Mariko. Her chest tightened with anger. "Put Fla . . . that kitten down! You're hurting him!" she shouted.

Lucy glared at Olivia. "What are you stressing about, Beanpole? It's not your kitten!"

Yes, he is! Olivia wanted to shout, but even now she knew that she couldn't tell them that. "Give him to me or else!" she demanded, rushing forward with clenched fists.

"Run for it!" Lucy shouted to Mariko, zooming across the lawn.

Olivia ran after her, her long legs eating up the grass.

Lucy glanced fearfully over her shoulder and then stopped abruptly at the well. She dangled Flame over the widely spaced bars covering the opening above the empty, black space.

"Back off! Or I'll drop him in!" she shouted.

Olivia froze. "You wouldn't!" she gasped.

Lucy's blue eyes glittered. "Don't you come any closer. Weird things happen when you're around!"

Flame's back legs pedalled the air. He screeched loudly with fear.

"Please don't hurt him!" Olivia begged. "Look, I just want the kitten. I didn't mean to lose my temper with you," she said reasonably.

"Give him to her, Lucy," Mariko urged. "Let her go and find out who it belongs to. Then we can go inside and watch the video."

"Shut up! Both of you!" Lucy snapped.

Olivia gulped. Lucy had a hard, mean look on her face. She looked capable of anything. Olivia's mind whirled. What could she do? "I'll . . . I'll make a deal with you," she blurted out. "I'll give you my ballet book for the kitten!"

Lucy wavered. "Really? Swear on this kitten's life that you'll let me keep the book."

"Okay. I swear," Olivia said solemnly.

"You heard that, Mariko!" Lucy crowed. She looked back at Olivia. "You have to keep your promise now or we'll tell everyone that you're a liar and a cheat."

Olivia didn't care. She felt weak with relief. "Whatever. You can go and get the book yourself. It's in the cabinet next to my bed."

Lucy backed slowly away from the well. "Here!" She thrust Flame into Olivia's arms. "I was only kidding, anyway! I hope it takes you hours to find its owner. Come on, Mariko. I'm going to the dormitory to get *my* book!" She ran off, followed by Mariko.

Olivia held Flame's little, trembling body to her chest. His tiny heart was beating fast against her hands. "It's okay, Flame. You're safe now," she crooned softly.

"Thank you for saving me, Olivia." Flame gave an especially loud purr and reached up a tiny paw to pat her cheek. "I am very sorry that you have lost your book."

"It doesn't matter. You're more

important to me than any old book. I nearly died on the spot when I thought Lucy was going to drop you into that well!" Olivia said.

She realized that she would do anything to protect Flame.

Chapter *EIGHT*

"We're collecting our costumes for the dress rehearsal onstage this morning!" Olivia swept Flame into her arms and shot down the stairs to the wardrobe department. "Can you believe that the performance is only the day after tomorrow?"

Flame shook his head. "I have been here with you for a few weeks now. The time has gone by very fast."

"I assume your uncle's spies have given up looking for you. Maybe you can stay here with me forever," Olivia said.

Flame looked up at her with gentle, green eyes. "That is not possible, Olivia. My destiny is in my own world."

"I know," Olivia said sadly. She didn't even want to think about Flame leaving.

Tamsin was already in the wardrobe department when Olivia and Flame arrived. "It's amazing in here, isn't it?" Tamsin said, pointing to the huge rolls of satins, chiffons, and velvets in every color imaginable.

Olivia quickly put Flame down on a bench, before Tamsin noticed that she seemed to be holding something that she couldn't see! He scampered past a woman sitting at a sewing machine and then settled down to watch another woman, hand sewing sequins on to a sky blue tutu.

Olivia caught her breath when she saw her costume. It had a pale orchid, silk bodice, with thin straps trimmed with tiny, pink rosebuds. The stiff skirt was held out by many layers of cream net. Her headdress was a band of matching pink rosebuds and crystal beads.

"Oh! It's even more beautiful than I expected," she sighed, holding it up against her.

Tamsin was cradling her pale gray costume in her arms. "Mine's gorgeous, too. I can't wait for dress rehearsal!"

The rest of the class collected their costumes and then everyone trooped along to the school's theater, where Miss Frances was waiting.

"Wow! Look at this!" Olivia said, peering around the stage.

Everything was almost ready for the main performance. There was a dark blue backcloth, with tiny lights for stars. The colorful scenery had been painted to look like the inside of a fairy-tale castle.

The dress rehearsal was exciting, but very hard work, as Miss Frances was even more strict than usual. Olivia concentrated fully on getting every step right. If she even started thinking about dancing in front of a full audience, her tummy did a sickening backflip.

When the rehearsal was over, Miss Frances gave a small smile. "That went really well. Go and get changed now. I'll see you this afternoon."

★

Olivia was practicing her pointe work at the barre as afternoon class began.

Tamsin joined her, starting some

warm-up stretches. "I just saw Lucy reading your ballet book in the common room. When I asked her about it, she said you gave it to her," she said, frowning.

Olivia nodded, feeling awful that she couldn't let Tamsin know why. "Yes, I did."

"How come? You can't stand her any more than I can!" Tamsin's eyes narrowed suspiciously. When Olivia looked away, she held up her hands. "Okay, you don't have to tell me anything. But I'll help you get your book back if you like."

"Thanks, Tamsin, but it doesn't matter now," Olivia said. She glanced across at the tiny ball of blue-gray fur on top of the piano. She still had what really mattered to her—Flame!

Miss Frances clapped her hands for attention. "Places, everyone. Let's go through the Garland Dance again. I want you all perfect for tomorrow."

As Olivia waited for the music to begin, the door of the studio opened. A frail-looking elderly woman, with black hair and a silver walking stick, came in.

Miss Frances quickly fetched a chair for her.

"It's Nina Svetlova!" Tamsin whispered. "She founded this school!"

"She must be going to take class!" Olivia guessed, glancing at the almost legendary ex-prima ballerina.

Nina banged on the floor with her stick. "Begin!" she ordered. She watched everyone closely, making corrections when she thought they were needed. "No, no! It's not meant to be like that!" she said, pointing her stick at Lucy. "You are too stiff. Move your arms like this. Hold up your head and smile!"

Lucy pressed her mouth together as she danced. Her face was beet red.

Then Nina turned her attention to Olivia. Olivia danced for all she was worth, trying not to think about the sharp, critical eyes watching her.

"Good!" said Nina, when Olivia

finished. "That is how the dance should be! You!" she said, pointing to Lucy. "Watch and learn!"

There were hushed whispers as the class ended and everyone went to get changed. Mariko had her arm around Lucy, who was in tears.

"Phew! I thought Miss Frances was strict, but she's got nothing on Miss Svetlova," Olivia said to Tamsin. "She must have made us do the Garland Dance about a hundred times! And she really grilled Lucy! I couldn't help feeling sorry for her."

Tamsin shrugged. "It's her own fault. She should make more of an effort." She flashed Olivia a pleased grin. "But I think we both did okay!"

Olivia nodded, feeling a flush of pride. She was going to call her parents as soon as she could and tell them that the famous Nina Svetlova had just coached her!

Chapter *NINE*

Olivia woke up the following morning with butterflies in her tummy. "This is the day! Mom and Dad will be on their way here soon," she said to Flame. "It's the final dress rehearsal this morning."

She jumped out of bed and got dressed quickly. Usually Flame followed her everywhere, but today he seemed reluctant to get off the bed.

"Hey! Sleepyhead," she teased gently. "Are you coming?"

Flame peeped out of his cozy nest in

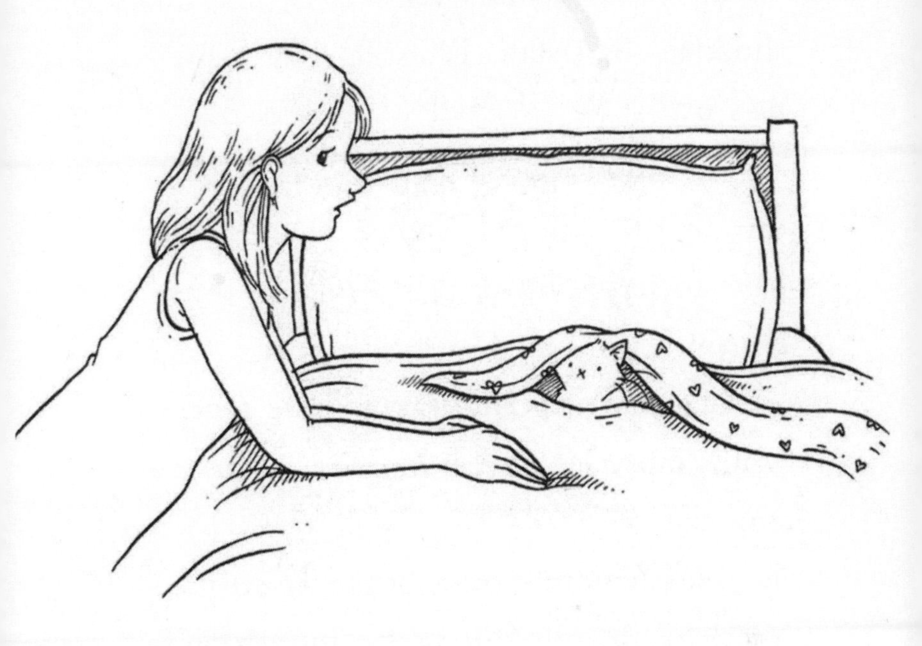

the duvet with dull, troubled eyes. "I think I will stay here for a bit longer," he meowed quietly.

"What's wrong? Do you feel sick?" Olivia asked, beginning to feel alarmed.

"I think my enemies are getting close," Flame told her with a tiny shudder. "If I stay very still, they may pass by."

"Oh, no!" Olivia gasped. She was dreading the moment when Flame would have to leave, but it was a million times worse to think of him being hurt. "That's it. I'm going to stay here with you. I'll say I have a tummy ache or something . . ."

"No. It would draw attention to me. You cannot miss this important rehearsal," Flame meowed.

Olivia knew Flame was right, but she felt torn. "All right, I'll go. But I'll come back and check on you when I can. You *will* still be here when I get back, won't you?" She was distraught at the thought of not being able to say good-bye.

Flame curled up and tucked his tail around his tiny body. He gave a muffled, little meow. "I hope so."

Olivia's heart was heavy as she went to the dance studio.

"Are you okay?" asked Tamsin, as soon as she caught sight of Olivia's pale face.

"Yes, I'm fine," Olivia said, trying hard to pull herself together.

She managed to push her worries about Flame to the back of her mind and somehow concentrated fully on her dancing, but the moment rehearsal finished, Olivia dashed straight back up to the dorm.

Flame was on the landing, ears pricked

and his little tail sticking straight up perkily. The fearful look had faded from his emerald eyes. He meowed a greeting as Olivia bounded up the stairs two at a time toward him.

"Flame!" Olivia cried happily. "I was so scared that you'd be gone!"

"I sensed that my enemies have passed. They may still return, but for now I am safe," Flame purred.

"Oh, I'm so glad!" Olivia bent down to stroke his soft fur. "Come on. It's almost lunchtime. I'll see if I can smuggle something extra delicious out for you!"

With a joyful little meow, Flame jumped into her arms.

★

Olivia sat in the common room with

Tamsin. Flame was curled up invisibly by her side. Normal lessons had finished early and the entire school seemed to be in upheaval as final preparations for the performance were made.

Olivia felt so nervous that she couldn't sit still. She kept jumping up and pacing around. Flame seemed to have been infected by her nerves. One minute he was sitting down, the next he was pacing behind her.

"What time is it?" Olivia asked Tamsin.

Tamsin grinned. "Five minutes later than when you just asked me!"

"Sorry," Olivia said. "I hate waiting around. If only there was something to do."

"We're supposed to be relaxing,"

Tamsin said. "There's still over an hour before we need to start putting on our makeup and costumes."

"It's no good. I feel like I have butterflies in my tummy! I think I'll go and see if Mom and Dad have arrived."

"Good idea," Tamsin said. "You must be dying to see them after all these weeks. Not like me; I have to see my parents every day. I'll stay here and read my magazine. I'll see you in wardrobe later."

"Okay," Olivia sang out as she hurried

out of the common room. She couldn't understand how Tamsin could be so calm when she was exactly the opposite!

With Flame in her shoulder bag, Olivia went outside to check the car park, but there was no sign of her parents' car yet.

"Never mind. They'll be here soon," she said to Flame. "Let's go back inside."

Flame answered with a sleepy purr from the depths of the bag.

Olivia put her hand inside and stroked Flame gently. She wandered down the corridor and found herself heading down toward the wardrobe room. Maybe she'd go and take another look at her costume.

Just before she got to wardrobe, she saw that the door to a normally empty room stood wide open. It was crammed with dress rails full of glittering costumes.

"Oh, look!" Olivia said delightedly, spotting her costume on the end of the rail nearest to her.

But as she reached for the hanger, Olivia caught a movement from the corner of her eye. A large, dark shadow was climbing the wall of the corridor. Something was coming toward them.

"He is close. I can sense him," growled a harsh, cruel voice.

Olivia froze. Flame's enemies. They were here!

Chapter *TEN*

Olivia didn't hesitate. She turned on her heel and ran. There was a coatroom just past wardrobe. As soon as she reached it, she hurtled inside.

"Flame! You must go! Now!" she hissed, opening her bag. "I just saw your uncle's spies. They're right behind us!"

Flame gave a startled meow and jumped out of her bag. His fur all stood on end and his ears were flattened. A flash of bright white light filled the whole coatroom and Olivia felt a shower of sparks come down all around her.

She blinked, half blinded. When she looked again, Flame had gone.

Olivia stood there, stunned. She couldn't believe what had just happened. Flame had left her without even saying good-bye!

She went back into the hallway in a daze and walked slowly back toward the room with the rails of costumes.

Lucy and Mariko were there now, collecting their costumes. Olivia frowned. She seemed to remember that Lucy's costume was pale violet, so why was she holding up a pale orchid tutu? As Olivia drew nearer, Mariko spotted her. She gave a start and nudged Lucy, who whipped around with a guilty expression on her face.

It was a moment before Olivia noticed the scissors in Lucy's hand. And then she saw the two big cuts on the bodice of her beautiful tutu.

Olivia gasped in disbelief at her ruined costume. There was a tight feeling in her chest, but instead of feeling angry, she just felt sad and weary. Flame had gone and she still couldn't really take that in. Hot tears began spilling down her face.

Mariko's face crumpled, too. "I'm really sorry," she murmured.

Lucy dropped the costume and the scissors. "I was only going to cut the rosebuds off. The scissors slipped . . ."

she said in a shaky voice. "You . . . you won't tell Miss Frances, will you? I'll get expelled."

"Just go away and leave me alone!" Olivia sobbed.

Lucy's lips trembled. She turned and ran off as fast as she could. Mariko hesitated, looking at Olivia like she wanted to say something, but then she turned and hurried after Lucy.

Olivia picked up her ruined costume. There was no time to repair it, even if it were possible to mend the damage. She couldn't dance in the performance now.

Suddenly her spine began to tingle. She heard a crackle of sparks and slowly turned around.

"Flame!" Olivia cried, as his tiny blue-gray form crawled out from under the dress rail. "You're still here! How? What?"

Flame's emerald eyes glittered. "I have laid a false scent trail. But my enemies are still close. I cannot stay for long."

She threw herself to her knees and picked him up. She thought her heart might burst with happiness. "Oh, I'm so happy you came back!"

"I wanted to be here to see you dance," he meowed solemnly, rubbing the top of his furry, little head against her cheek.

"But how can . . ." Olivia began, looking down at the slashed bodice of her tutu.

Flame lifted his paw and a fine sprinkle of silver sparks shot out. They drifted on to the tutu like glittering talcum powder. The rips in the bodice edges drew together by themselves and the slashes faded slowly, until the only thing Olivia

could see was the pale glint of the silky-smooth fabric.

She held up the tutu. “It’s as good as new,” she said delightedly. “Oh, Flame. Thank you so much.”

“You are welcome. I think it is time for you to get ready now!” Flame meowed, showing his little, sharp teeth in a grin.

Olivia stood on the stage next to Tamsin. Her mind was a blank. She felt sure that she had forgotten every step that Miss Frances had taught her.

Her heart beat fast as the first bars of the Garland Dance began. Slowly, the curtain was raised.

Olivia took a deep breath and began dancing.

Her feet seemed to move by themselves as she drifted lightly across the stage, in perfect time with the other dancers. In the bright light, the stage set was a glittering fairy realm. Olivia danced with her heart and soul, losing herself completely in the spirit of the dance. All too soon the music began to fade and she swept into a graceful bow.

The audience broke into enthusiastic applause.

Olivia quickly glanced at the delighted faces, trying to spot her parents. With so many rows of seats, she couldn't see them, but she was sure they were there somewhere.

The music changed and Olivia glided on a cloud of happiness into the wings with the other girls.

As soon as they were backstage, Tamsin ran over and gave her a hug. "How amazing was that?" she cried.

"It was incredible! Like a dream," Olivia said.

Miss Frances appeared from the shadows. "Good job!" she said, giving them both a hug. "I'm very proud of you both."

Olivia and Tamsin were too shocked to speak. *Wonders would never cease*, Olivia thought, biting back a grin. *Miss Frances seemed almost human.*

"I've got some wonderful news. Nina Svetlova was very impressed when she saw you in class the other day. She's recommended that you both move up a class next semester!" Miss Frances said.

"That's fantastic!" Tamsin said. She grabbed Olivia and they jumped up and down with their mouths open in silent squeals of excitement.

Lucy suddenly appeared with Mariko

backstage. "I still don't know how she repaired the costume so quickly . . ." Olivia heard her whispering.

But when she saw Olivia and Tamsin with Miss Frances, Lucy stopped. Her eyes flickered worriedly between Olivia and the teacher. "What . . . what are you talking to Miss Frances about?" she asked sweetly.

Olivia knew that Lucy thought she was snitching.

"Not everything's about you, Lucy. You tell them our news, Tamsin!" Olivia called over her shoulder, already rushing off to find Flame.

She couldn't wait to tell him the amazing news!

Olivia ran into the shadows of the

prop room at the back of the stage, but before she could even speak, there was a blinding silver flash and a shower of sparks. A regal, young, white lion stood looking solemnly at Olivia. An older, gray lion stood next to him.

Flame raised his big, white paw in farewell and Olivia knew that his trick to escape his enemies had been discovered. This time, Flame was leaving for good.

"Be well, be strong, and dance with a brave heart, Olivia," Flame rumbled in a deep, velvety voice. And then he and the older lion vanished.

"I'll never forget you, Flame," Olivia whispered, her heart aching. But at least she had been able to see him one more time. She knew she would always remember her wonderful magic kitten.

"Olivia, sweetie!" called a voice. "We just got here in time to see the performance. You were fantastic!"

She looked up and saw her parents standing backstage, beaming with pride.

"Mom! Dad! I've got some amazing news!" Olivia called, running toward them.

Read all of the books
in the Magic Kitten series!

A tiny orange kitten needs a friend!
Magic Kitten
A Summer Spell
SUE BENTLEY

A fluffy black-and-white kitten needs a friend!
Magic Kitten
Classroom Chaos
SUE BENTLEY

A tan kitten needs a friend!
Magic Kitten
Star Dreams
SUE BENTLEY

A white Christmas kitten needs a friend!
Magic Kitten
A Christmas Surprise
SUE BENTLEY

A sweet silver tabby kitten needs a friend!
Magic Kitten
Double Trouble
SUE BENTLEY

Magic Kitten
Moonlight Mischief
SUE BENTLEY

An adorable coal-black kitten needs a friend!
Magic Kitten
A Circus Wish
SUE BENTLEY

A velvety blue-grey kitten needs a friend!
Magic Kitten
Sparkling Steps
SUE BENTLEY

Read all of the books
in the Magic Puppy series!

A tiny golden retriever puppy needs a friend!
Magic Puppy
A New Beginning
SUE BENTLEY

A tiny border collie puppy needs a friend!
Magic Puppy
Muddy Paws
SUE BENTLEY

A tiny Jack Russell puppy needs a friend!
Magic Puppy
Cloud Capers
SUE BENTLEY

A tiny spaniel puppy needs a friend!
Magic Puppy
Star of the Show
SUE BENTLEY

A tiny Dalmatian puppy needs a friend!
Magic Puppy
Party Dreams
SUE BENTLEY

A tiny West Highland terrier puppy needs a friend!
Magic Puppy
A Forest Charm
SUE BENTLEY

A tiny Border Terrier puppy needs a friend!
Magic Puppy
Twirling Tails
SUE BENTLEY

A tiny English Sheepdog puppy needs a friend!
Magic Puppy
School of Mischief
SUE BENTLEY

About the Author

Sue Bentley's books for children often include animals or fairies. She lives in Northampton and enjoys reading, going to the movies, and sitting watching the frogs and newts in her garden pond. If she hadn't been a writer, she would probably have been a skydiver or a brain surgeon. The main reason she writes is that she can drink pots and pots of tea while she's typing. She has met and owned many cats and each one has brought a special sort of magic to her life.